The TRAIN Who Was Frightened of the Dark

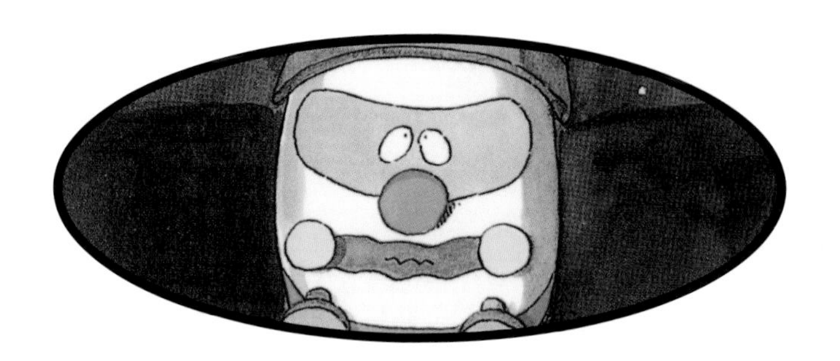

Denis Bond

Illustrated by

Valeria Petrone

Coach
House

Look out for more great titles
by Denis Bond and Valeria Petrone

The Dragon Who Couldn't Help Breathing Fire

The Granny Who Wasn't Like Other Grannies

The Monster Who Couldn't Scare Anyone

The Witch Who Loved to Make Children Cry

The Shark Who Bit Things He Shouldn't

Further copies of this book or other books in the series are available from Coach House Publications Ltd

You can also order on line from
www.coachhouseonline.co.uk

Coach House Publications Ltd
The Coach House,
School Green Road,
Freshwater,
Isle of Wight
PO40 9BB

First published in the UK in 1992 by
Scholastic Children's Books

This edition published in 2003 by
Coach House Publications Ltd

ISBN 1-899-392-22X

Printed in the UK

In a cosy, wooden shed in the middle of the countryside lived a train. During the daytime he was a very happy, little train.

But at night, the train wasn't happy at all. As soon as it got dark he began to get scared. The little train was frightened of the dark. He knew it was silly, but he couldn't help it.

Every night he would open the door to his shed so that the moonlight could make everything bright. The cold wind made the little train shiver, but he didn't mind. He would rather be cold than frightened.

Early one morning, the little train pulled up at the village station. There were lots of passengers waiting and they all scrambled aboard. They wanted to go into the big town, where most of them worked.

The little train set off on his journey, travelling very gently along the railway track.
CLICKETY-CLACK!
CLICKETY-CLACK!
As he passed the cornfield, the passengers waved to the scarecrow.
The scarecrow smiled and waved back.

Suddenly there was a loud SCREECH! Sparks flew up from the little train's wheels as he skidded to a halt at the entrance to a dark tunnel. The little train hated tunnels.

Inside the tunnel, it was very, very dark. "I can't go in there," thought the little train. "It's probably full of spiders and bats."

"There might be monsters!" he said. "Or even ghosts!"

The little train was very, very frightened.

“I’ll go a different way to the town,” he decided, and he turned away from th tunnel and sped across the cornfield. The terrified scarecrow leapt out of his way.

And the farmer called out, angrily, “Get out of my cornfield, you naughty little train!”

The ride across the cornfield was a bumpy one and the passengers began bouncing out of their seats.
One old lady was enjoying every minute of it.
"Wheee!" she laughed.

But the rest of the passengers were very unhappy. A little boy's ice-cream cone landed on his dad's nose. And a baby's bottle flew into the air, showering everyone with sticky orange-juice. "Ugh!" they all shouted.

Having reached the foot of a very tall mountain, the little train began his steep climb to the top.

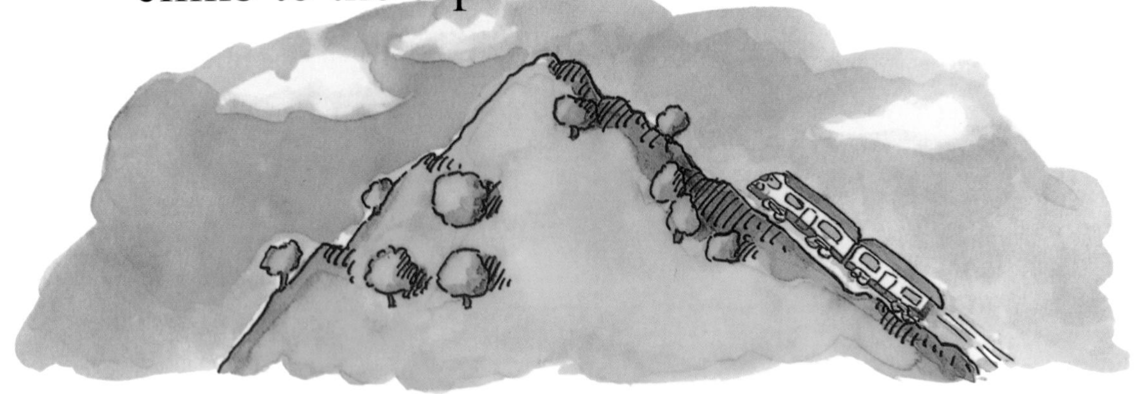

The passengers gazed silently out of the windows.
"Oh dear!" gasped one terrified lady.
"What a long drop!"

The little train arrived at the top of the mountain and then sped down the other side.
"Too fast! Too fast!" the passengers screamed as hats and bags and umbrellas flew through the carriage windows.

"Wheee!" shouted the old lady.

The little train came to a stream which was crossed by a rickety, wooded bridge. "I'm not crossing over that!" said a young man. He took off his shoes, rolled up his trousers and paddled across the stream.

As the little train crossed the bridge, it began to shake from side to side. Pieces of wood began to splinter and soon the bridge started to fall apart.

The little train had just managed to reach the other side of the stream when the whole bridge crumbled and tumbled into the water with a loud SPLASH!

The little train then rushed through the park, scattering all the children from their playground.

His metal wheels churned up the sand-pit, throwing sand everywhere, which covered all the passengers from head to foot.

Soon, the little train arrived in the town. All the shoppers were horrified to see a train hurtling down their busy high street.

Cars and taxis and buses all screeched to a halt.
The little train had caused a traffic jam and there was a deafening sound as all the drivers sounded their horns.

As soon as they heard the noise, police cars came rushing from the police station.

And fire engines came rushing from the fire station.

And that made the traffic jam even worse.

Much later, the little train arrived at the station. All the passengers tumbled out of the carriages and hurried to their offices, banks and shops.
"You've made us late for work!" they all shouted, angrily.

At the end of the day, the passengers decided not to travel home on the railway.
Some travelled by ferry-boat.

Some travelled by bus.

Some of them travelled by taxi and some decided to walk home.

One very rich passenger travelled home by helicopter and as he passed over the station, he shook his fist angrily at the little train. The little train was very upset.

Only one passenger arrived at the station
to be taken home by the little train.
It was the old lady.
"I hope this journey is going to be as
exciting as this morning's journey,"
she laughed.

The little train had caused enough fuss for one day, so he decided to travel home the proper way.

But when he came to the dark tunnel, he couldn't go any further.
"I'm frightened of the dark," he cried.

"Well, put your lights on, you silly train!" said the old lady.
The little train hadn't thought of doing that! He switched on his lights and he could see right through the tunnel to the opening at the other end.

As he travelled through the tunnel, the little train could see there was nothing to be frightened of.
There were a few spiders.
There were a few bats.
But none of them took any notice of the little train.

"And there's no such things as ghosts!" laughed the old lady as they pulled up at the village station. "No such things as ghosts and no such things as monsters!" The old lady had found the journey very dull, but she knew that all the other passengers would have enjoyed it.

The following morning, the village station was crowded with waiting passengers. The old lady had told them all that the little train was no longer frightened of the dark. The little train was very happy to see everyone scramble aboard.

That night, the door of the wooden shed was shut tight. The little train switched his lights on. And off.
And on.
And off.
Then he went to sleep. There was nothing to be frightened of.